MY THINK-A-MA-JINK

Written and illustrated by

DAVE WHAMOND

Owl kids

To my parents, who always inspired me to use my imagination and
to the real life Zac and Maria, who inspire me with their imaginations every day!

Owlkids Books Inc.
10 Lower Spadina Avenue, Suite 400, Toronto, Ontario M5V 2Z2
www.owlkids.com

Distributed in Canada by University of Toronto Press
5201 Dufferin Street, Toronto, Ontario M3H 5T8

Distributed in the United States by Publishers Group West
1700 Fourth Street, Berkeley, California 94710

Library and Archives Canada Cataloguing in Publication

Whamond, Dave
My think-a-ma-jink / written and illustrated by Dave Whamond

Issued also in electronic format.
ISBN 978-1-897349-66-3 (bound).--ISBN 978-1-926973-10-4 (pbk.)

I. Title.

PS8645.H34M9 2009 jC813'.6 C2009-900997-8

Library of Congress Control Number: 2009923336

E-book ISBN: 978-1-926818-51-1

Canada Council for the Arts / Conseil des Arts du Canada
ONTARIO ARTS COUNCIL
CONSEIL DES ARTS DE L'ONTARIO

We acknowledge the financial support of the Canada Council for the Arts, the Government of Canada through the Canada Book Fund, the Ontario Arts Council, and the Ontario Media Development Corporation.

Manufactured by Sheck Wah Tong Printing Press Ltd.
Manufactured in Guang Dong, China in August 2011
Job #55499

A B C D E F

Publisher of Chirp, chickaDEE and OWL
www.owlkids.com

My name is Jack.
I am bored.

Today was my birthday and I wasn't even that excited. I kept getting toys that did everything for me.

But later that night, my sister Marie brought me a present. I must have missed it at the party. The tag said: "*From Uncle Doug.*" Strange. I didn't even know I HAD an Uncle Doug.

We opened the box to find a wonderfully weird contraption. It looked broken, but shone like it was brand new.

We found a note, too. It read:

"The Think-a-ma-Jink—an imagination machine. Be anything! Go anywhere! All you have to do is dream."

A

"I'll believe THAT when I see it,"
I thought as I went to bed.

But I couldn't sleep. That glowing
Think-a-ma-Jink kept me awake.

I needed to try it out.

The instructions said:
"Relax, open your mind,
and repeat the words: THINK
THINK
THINK-A-MA-JINK
HULLA-BA-LOO
RAZZA-MA-
DOO..."

Boy, did I feel silly. Especially when…

nothing happened!

Just like I thought.

Nope. Nothing. At. All…

Suddenly, I was a freakish mutant monster
attacking an unsuspecting city.
Cool, I've always wanted to do that!

SALE
Try THIS
ROXY

Maybe this thing really worked after all.
All I had to do was think...

And it worked again. The box changed into a hot air balloon!

This Think-a-ma-Jink could do anything! Like take us to distant corners of the universe to meet far-out crazy aliens.

We could travel to
a time before there
were any humans.

Yikes!

Or I could be a pirate
saving a fair maiden from
a cotton-candy-breathing
dragon. Look out!

I know, I know…it's usually a KNIGHT saving a fair maiden from a FIRE-breathing dragon. But it's MY Think-a-ma-Jink. I can do what I like.

We could even go to Lollipop-palooza, where everything was gooey and delicious!

The only part I didn't like
was getting toffee stuck
between my toes.

We were about to reach the peak of Mount Everfudge when I made the mistake of letting Marie carry the Think-a-ma-Jink.

She turned me into the Abominable Snowman!
Although I like being called "Yeti" better.

Just for that, I turned her into Frogzilla!

So she turned me into Princess Stinkerbell.

Then I changed her into a Scottish Gargyle!

We were so busy turning each other into crazy creatures that we didn't notice...

...my Think-a-ma-Jink got knocked into the air...

...and smashed into a **million bajillion pieces!**

This couldn't be happening!

Not the Think-a-ma-Jink!

What about my adventures?

What should I do?

I had to think!

Think, Jack, think...

It worked! I actually did it

all by myself!

And if I could do **THAT**...

...then I could imagine

anything!

The End

(actually it was just the beginning)